WHEN YOU HEAR IT…

THE SOUND

AN AOTEAROA HORROR STORY

The Sound: An Aotearoa Horror Story

Edited by Danielle Yeager, Hack & Slash Editing

Book Cover by Ruth Anna Evans

Layout by Joseph Stephen Bonnett

ISBN: 978-1-0670709-6-0

www.jsbonnett.com

The Sound: An Ambient Musical Score

Dear reader, if you enjoy ambient music, I have composed a short musical score inspired by this story. Please use the QR codes or links below to access it. The files can be downloaded for free via Bandcamp, or email **jsbonnett@outlook.com** if you would like free MP3 or WAV files; I would be happy to send them.

YouTube

https://youtu.be/xS0hCtlbdHo?si=6s6Hp6nK1r0bjKLr

Bandcamp

https://josephstephenbonnett.bandcamp.com/album/the-sound-an-aotearoa-horror-story-original-music-inspired-by-the-novella

1.

LISA SCRAMBLED OUT of the passenger's seat, breathing heavy, the sound of screeching tires still ringing out in her mind. She stood across from Ben, a dark pile on the ground at their feet. The car's high beams pierced the wet morning darkness between them, and through the steamy diffusion, Lisa watched her husband devolve into a helpless child, a deer in headlights—an impotent version of him she hadn't yet met until now, who seemed distant and drifting further away in his petulance. A fever dream remnant of a loved one turned alien and sour.

"It's not my fault," Ben said again in the tone of a guilty child.

Lisa just nodded, tired of his panicked monologue. She looked back at the road, concerned that the car jutted out from the gravel shoulder by Monkey Creek Bridge onto State Highway 94, which was narrow, winding and hazardous.

Expansive cliffs looked down on them from all around, the snow caps starting to peek through the bleak morning light. The air was crisp and fragrant with a trace of wet floral notes on a gentle breeze. The scene should have been idyllic but was wholly ruined by the dyspnoeic hissing from the badly injured albatross lying on the gravel between them. The giant bird had gone largely still, apart from an intermittent heaving of the chest as it struggled for air.

"Please, say something," Ben said to break the awkward silence. "It's not my fault."

"You need to calm down," Lisa replied.

"Calm down? We hit a fucking albatross."

"I know. So, like I have been saying, we should do something. The visitor's terminal is only forty minutes away; we can call for help. There must be a number for this sort of thing."

"I don't know . . . I'm not calling anyone. I'm pretty sure you can get in some serious shit for this. Aren't they protected?"

"It was an accident."

"I'm not risking it."

"So what are you going to do? We can't just leave it like this."

"Why me? We're in this together."

"I told you what I think we should do."

Ben dragged his sneaker across the gravel, kicking up small dust clouds. Ten days into their honeymoon and all he could think of was how he had screwed up at every opportunity: Thirteen hours at the back of the plane next to the toilets that opened every two minutes because he forgot to pick the seats. A nine-hour layover at the Kuala Lumpur airport because he misread the booking. Poorly planned long stretches of driving between cheap and dank motels, leaving little time for much else other than missed exits, wrong turns, and arguments about where to eat. And now, he had been speeding—not paying attention—and wiped out a magnificent, rare, and protected bird.

"Ben?" Lisa snapped.

"Just get in the car and don't look," he replied.

"Fine."

She got in and slammed the door behind her. The thought that perhaps she actually didn't like her husband very much crossed her mind, but she forcefully attributed it to the fatigue and the stress. They had spent too much time driving and the road was conducive to arguments, but it had also revealed a fragility to Ben, that the twenty-eight-year-old had a tendency to crack under pressure.

Despite his instructions not to, she watched her husband's frantic figure, obscured through the fogged-up window. He finally moved with a sense of purpose as he circled the bird, grabbed a leg, and then dragged it across the gravel the last few feet to the ridge of the creek bank. He circled again and then gracelessly kicked the declining albatross down the slope with a weak leg and a laboured grunt. The scene was disturbing; Ben's hunched and slender frame made him look ghoul-like, just a black shape performing ugly actions in the dark. Lisa cringed in disapproval as the bird scraped down the start of the hill by the small concrete bridge, accompanied by the sound of dragging gravel, and then a dull *thud* as it came to rest farther down. Ben scrambled after it, disappearing down the short but steep slope.

"Ben!" she yelled out the open window.

There was no reply and the world fell silent. A moment later came the distant droning of a vehicle somewhere along the highway, in the hills behind them.

"Ben, what are you doing?" she yelled, louder this time.

A head appeared over the top of the bank.

"It's dead," he said, scrambling up on all fours.

"It looked alive," she countered.

"It was . . . now it's dead. There's nothing more we could have done."

He got in the car and slammed the driver's door behind him, filling the space with a sour panic-fuelled perspiration.

The beginning of a burnt orange sunrise crested the peaks to their left and in the emerging light, the deep grooves in the gravel where the bird had been pulled became an obvious crime scene— gaping channels of dark wet gravel, black compared to the drier surface material. Lisa went to mention it and thought better than to set Ben off. As he pulled off the shoulder onto the highway with a heavy foot—apparently not at all tentative or dulled by the event—distant headlights breached the wooded corner down the hill behind them.

The crisp and clear early morning had switched aggressively as they arrived at the Milford Sound Visitor's Terminal. The rain seemed to come out of nowhere and hammer down on the sunbaked docks before the gloom caught up with it.

The bus in front of them pulled into a designated coach area, and Ben floored the accelerator in frustration for the remaining two-second journey to a free space. He had been cursing the bus for at least twenty minutes as he was unable to pass it on the winding blind corners of Milford Sound Road.

Hordes of visitors milled around the parking lot, gathering belongings and hurrying each other in the rain.

They walked the short walk to the terminal along the gravel path, then under the trees along the boardwalk. After checking in at the building, they exited the other side to the slick wooden dock.

"That one, wharf number six," Ben said, pointing with one hand while shielding his eyes from a non-existent sun with the other.

While her parents arranged backpacks on the ground, a young girl of maybe seven or eight skipped in circles in the middle of the path and sang, "Water, water, everywhere, but not a drop to drink." The couple skirted the group.

"Sorry," said Lisa, unsure why she was apologising for the family taking up space.

"Water, water, everywhere . . ." The young girl continued, and her even younger brother joined in, chasing her in circles and mumbling his own toddlerised version in mimicry.

"Don't run, you'll fall off the dock," the father yelled.

"Better not be on our boat," Ben muttered, safely out of range.

They arrived at wharf six and boarded the boat hand in hand, rain beating on their black ponchos they'd purchased from the visitor's terminal. A huddle of other passengers led the way, some in matching ponchos, others in coloured windbreakers. All marched on with hoods up—a cult of precipitation.

Grey and murky water surged underneath the gangway. The filthy foamed edges spat up the sides of the pilings—industrial, discoloured, and angry compared to the pristine waters farther out. The rain did its best to dilute the filth with heavy drops that punched holes in the water's surface, as the heights of the Southern Alps demanded the tepid winds return their bounty to the Tasman Sea. The weather was powerful and beautiful, inspiring awe and a little anxiety as Ben and Lisa looked to the sky and let the rain wash away some of the fatigue. Lisa thought back to what the ticketing agent had said earlier, *The heavy weather was the best way to see Piopiotahi. The true Milford Sound experience, the rugged West Coast.*

At the end of the gangway, the *Milford Guardian* bobbed heavily in the weather—a twenty-eight-metre motor cruiser with front, back, and upper-level observation decks, and a restaurant, bar, and lounge that opened to the front deck and bow.

Ben turned to Lisa, strands of his short and scruffy black hair pasted to his narrow forehead and dripping onto a wide and childlike grin. "Not too many people. I was worried it would be crowded . . . and with kids."

Lisa looked around and counted only seven other passengers and the three crew members. She put her arm around Ben and smiled a smile that still wore the earlier drama on its unconvincing edges.

"Thank you," she said. "This was a wonderful idea."

Their cabin was tight, just a double bed that barely fit and a small bathroom off the side. But two rectangular windows looked out to the stunningly glassy, kyanite water. Rows of empty wharfs lined up across the harbour before the long wooden boardwalk gave way to the mountains that reached up to the clouds.

Ben stood at the window and looked towards the parking lot for their rental car, but it was too far away and obscured by trees. He had forgotten to check the front of the vehicle for any traces of the accident and hoped the heavy rain would clean any blood and bits away. Still, he couldn't shake the thought of the car telling secrets.

Water beaded off their ponchos and hit the thick carpet where dark grey patches formed around their feet. They stripped and hung their rain gear on a hook on the back of the door. The soaking wet ends of Lisa's long red hair painted her sweater, and small mascara trails ran from both eyes.

Ben surveyed the room. "Not bad. Check the fridge."

Lisa opened the small bar fridge jammed in the corner and pulled out two single-serve bottles of sparkling wine.

"Class," Ben said.

"Should we save them?" Lisa asked.

"For what? Crack 'em open."

As she opened the second bottle and poured, the boat vibrated and started up. They raised their glasses. The landscape shifted as the *Milford Guardian* pulled away from the harbour, and the empty docks gave way to mountains.

"Here we go," Ben said and emptied his glass.

2.

THEY SPENT THE day cruising through Piopiotahi. They watched dolphins racing alongside the boat, seals lounging on cold wet rocks, and flocks of black billed gulls and blue ducks in the air and on the water. They ate, they drank, and they forgot about the morning's troubles. When night fell and the rain finally stopped, they poured rum into half-filled plastic Coke bottles and sat on the top deck, her head on his shoulder, his right hand on her thigh.

"It's beautiful," she said as they watched the moonlit Stirling Falls perform its work. Three separate water streams bridged the crest and coalesced into one powerful source before crashing onto the rocks and splitting off again into multiple waterfalls that plunged directly into the fiord.

They shared a brief silence while Lisa took a long sip from her bottle. She grimaced slightly at the potent mix and cleared her throat.

"Hey, so I saw a really interesting job listing yesterday."

"You were looking at job listings . . . on holiday? Jesus, Lisa, you don't know how to relax."

"I was just curious. I wanted to see what work is like here, in New Zealand, I mean."

"Right," Ben said.

"Are you going to ask me?"

"Ask you what?"

"About the job, Ben. I said I saw an interesting job."

He took a deep drink of his bottle and smirked at Lisa.

"Go on then, tell me," he said.

"Forget about it."

"No, come on, I'm sorry. I want to hear about it."

Lisa looked away from her husband, towards the waterfall. "Okay, well, it's in Auckland."

"I didn't like Auckland much."

"We were there for one day, Ben. Anyway, we have been talking about this for ages. You know I want to move out of London, and it's really interesting—it's a legal secretary job."

"So, exactly what you do at home, then?"

"Well, yeah, but they specialise in environmental law, which is what I want to do. I could go back to school part-time, see if I can finish my degree."

"Probably end up defending crooks, oil spills, and the like."

"You have no idea how the legal system works, do you?"

Ben ignored this in favour of his bottle.

"Can't you imagine me walking the room while I deliver my closing argument? I can." Lisa smiled. "Should I apply?"

"Seriously, can we just enjoy being on holiday?"

"Is that what we are doing, enjoying ourselves?" Lisa asked with a hint of spite.

Ben tensed his jaw.

"Sorry, I didn't mean that," she said.

"We don't have visas," Ben stated.

"But we can get them. I think. We can try at least."

"You really want to move here?" Ben asked.

"Maybe . . . yes. I think we would love it here."

"We could," Ben said in muted support.

"But?"

"No but. I said we could."

"We could . . . I would. Would you?"

"Sure . . . maybe."

She paused and gave him time to elaborate, but he just sipped his drink and looked at the waterfall.

Lisa continued. "I'm sick of spending every day in the same place, just going in circles. I need to shake things up."

"What if I can't find a job?"

"You'll find a job. Come on, let's make a plan," Lisa said.

"Now?"

"Yes, now. I want to sit here and drink and come up with something big and crazy. I want to look back years later and remember the time we got drunk on a boat on our honeymoon and decided to move here, or somewhere . . . anywhere."

Ben chewed his lip. He looked out at the water, then back at his wife. "Let's talk about it tomorrow."

Lisa slumped back into her seat. "Fine," she uttered.

The boat jumped, then dipped in the current. They heard someone banging around on the deck below just before the spotlights on top of the boat went dark. Neither stirred from their place on the bench.

"Did I just ruin the night?" Ben asked.

"No . . . it's okay. You're right, we can talk about it tomorrow."

"It's beautiful out here with the lights off. Look at the sky, it's so clear now, so full of stars," Ben said.

The sound of heavy water from Stirling Falls rang out in the distance. Nearer, down below, small waves slapped against the side of the boat, and ropes creaked.

Ben roughly brought his bottle to his lips, striking his bottom front teeth with the plastic rim. He threw his head back and emptied it, then blew out the heat of the strong mix into the cold air. He unzipped his pants, pulled it out, pressed the end of his limp member to the rim of the bottle, and started filling it.

"Fucking hell, Ben, are you kidding me?!" Lisa exclaimed.

"I'm not walking all the way back downstairs," he said over the sound of piss on plastic.

"What are you going to do with it? You're not bringing it back to the room."

"Roger that."

Ben zipped up and stood awkwardly, almost spilling urine on his hands. He walked to the edge of the deck and poured it out over the railing, the wind blowing much of it against the side of the boat. He stumbled back and sat down heavily next to Lisa.

They sat in silence for a moment. Behind them the thuds of flight approached, slow and powerful downstrokes of an audibly large wingspan, followed by a dull *splash* of a considerable body alighting on the water.

"You're an animal," Lisa said, and Ben laughed.

3.

BEN WOKE TO a thumping skull. Lisa was already up, sitting on the edge of the bed with a book in her hand but paying it no attention as she stared out the window.

"Morning," she said.

"Christ, what time is it?"

"Just after nine."

"It's early, can I go back to sleep?"

"I'm starving. I don't want to miss breakfast."

Ben huffed and pushed his thumb and index finger into his eyes.

"Okay, give me five minutes to shower."

He pulled his legs over the edge of the bed, knocking over an empty plastic Coke bottle and the half-full forty-ounce bottle of rum, then dragged himself to the shower. He stood under the water and let it pelt the back of his neck, wishing for more water pressure to break the tension and ease his headache. He struggled to piece together the final hours of last night and silently cursed for doing it to himself again.

Out of the shower, Ben saw Lisa popping painkiller tablets onto the nightstand.

"Get me a couple of those, too, please. My head is killing me," he said.

"I'm not surprised. You look like shit."

"Thank you, darling, just what I was hoping to hear."

"It's not my fault that one night on a boat has you swilling rum straight out of the bottle like some sort of nerdy-looking pirate."

"Straight out of the bottle? Fuck, I don't remember that."

Upstairs in the dining room, the morning sun had replaced last night's rain, and it cast shadows on a long table laid out with all kinds of food. Nearby, three girls who looked to be in their twenties sat with their breakfasts. They had had very little to do with them the day before, but Ben thought he recognised German as they spoke to each other. At another table sat Callum and Cecilia, the holidaying couple from Auckland they had befriended at the bar yesterday. Callum, a large man with a shaved head and stubbly grey beard, wore a short-sleeved pink shirt and grey golf shorts. Cecilia, a tall and slim woman with long, dark, curly hair and wearing a white summer dress, sipped orange juice.

Ben and Lisa grabbed their food and took the table next to Callum and Cecilia.

"You look like shit," Callum said to Ben.

"So everyone keeps telling me," Ben replied, then downed half a glass of orange juice.

Callum laughed and pulled a small folding pocketknife from his jacket. He unfolded the three-inch curved blade from the dark wooden handle and started cutting an apple into slices.

"Nice knife," Ben said.

"Huh? Oh, yeah, it was an anniversary present. To be honest, I forgot it was in my bag, but it comes in handy. You tried cutting an apple with a butter knife?"

Callum continued cutting, and Ben and Lisa sipped their coffee.

"Hey, did you guys hear that last night? Around two in the morning?" Callum asked the group, with a mouth full of apple slice.

"I didn't hear anything," Ben replied, earning him a slap on the arm from his wife.

"That sound, Ben . . . like a low rumbling . . . I woke you up," Lisa said.

"Really low . . . deep," Callum added. "It got right into you, like I could feel it in my stomach, then there was a high-pitched sort of squeal, I guess you would call it, and then it was over."

"I thought the boat was starting up for a second," Lisa replied, "but it was so alien, so weird. And then the high-pitched part at the end, how do you even describe it?"

"Like a dog repeller," Callum said.

"A dog repeller?" Lisa repeated.

"Yeah, a little handheld thing. Don't really see them around anymore, but you press a button and it makes a high-pitched noise, pisses dogs right off, and will send 'em running. To a human, it's just unpleasant, like an instant ringing in your ears. If you can hear it at all, that is. It gets harder as you get older."

"Fuck me, that's a random reference," Said Ben.

"They have apps for that sort of thing now," Cecilia pointed out.

"It made the birds go crazy," Lisa said. "You could hear them all calling out afterwards, like they were distressed. Which was odd, 'cause you don't normally hear birds at night, right?"

"It was weird, honestly," Callum agreed.

After breakfast the passengers gathered on the decks in the sun and in the crisp wind, as the boat moved towards the underwater observatory for their only scheduled "off-boat" activity. Ben and Lisa chose the back deck, drank more coffee, and watched the world from a wooden bench that gave them an unobstructed view of what they were leaving behind. Like ancient custodians, the mountains guided the boat through the channel as they left the mouth of the ocean and closed in on the observatory en route to the dock. The fiord curved so that in the distance the intercepting rock gave the illusion of being entirely contained as a lake rather than a passage to the Tasman Sea.

As they sat in silence, the choppy white wake painted a strip across the deep blue and captivated them until Ben felt a disturbance in his stomach. He initially thought it to be the culmination of motion and last night's alcohol, but it quickly became something else—a mixture of adrenaline, the dip of a rollercoaster, and somehow, comfortable nostalgia—a stirring from the scent of petrol and grass clippings.

A deep and undetermined groan that seemed to shake the world around the couple grew in intensity and overtook his senses. When violent gusts of wind slammed the vessel and the screeching hit his ears, Ben felt only intense fear. It passed quickly—two, maybe three seconds—and as the engine shifted and the boat slowed, Ben felt as if he had just awoken from sleep: disorientated, the remnants of a disturbing dream dissipating. The landscape looked different suddenly, like he had blacked out for a moment and come back farther along the fiord. A strange feeling of déjà vu overwhelmed him, like he had been here and done this before.

"There, what the hell was that?" Lisa asked, her right hand wrapped tightly around the sleeve of her husband's jacket.

"I don't know," Ben said, unable to articulate the sound or the feeling.

Muffled voices travelled from the front of the boat, dampened under the clamour of frenzied gulls circling overhead.

"Something's happening up there," Ben pointed out.

They got up and rounded the perimeter to the front deck. Everyone was gathered in their groups. There was a strange feeling of discontent in the air, and the couple was greeted with crossed arms.

"Are we at the observatory?" Ben asked no one in particular.

"We're lost," a middle-aged man whom Ben had not yet properly met answered from behind heavily tinted aviator sunglasses.

"What do you mean, 'We're lost'?" Ben asked.

But the man ignored him and turned back to his companion, a woman who also wore dark glasses above a contemptuous sneer and whispered something to him about being "too dramatic" that Ben couldn't entirely hear.

"Ben, did he just say we are lost'?" Lisa asked. "How is that even possible? There is nowhere to go but up and down the fiord."

"Right. I don't know what he's on about," Ben said.

One of the crew members, identifiable as *Jordy* from his name tag, moved through the passengers. "Aviators Guy," as Ben had now dubbed him, tapped Jordy heavily on the shoulder and gestured towards Ben and Lisa. "Tell them what you told us," he said and turned away.

Jordy looked momentarily stunned, but he plastered on a smile and addressed Ben and Lisa, "Kia ora, guys. Nothing to worry about, just a few issues with the navigational equipment. We're a little farther up the fiord than we thought . . . might be a little late for the observatory."

"Navigational equipment?" Ben repeated. "What is there to navigate? You go out to sea, you turn around, and you come back."

"We're just a bit farther out than expected," Jordy explained.

Behind him, the German girls talked among themselves and looked as relaxed as they did at breakfast. One of them said something behind a raised hand and they all laughed. Callum and Cecilia were standing on the other side of the deck, looking over into the water.

"What was that noise?" Lisa asked Jordy.

"What noise is that?" he answered as he half turned to leave.

Lisa paused, surprised she had to elaborate. "The low sound, the uh, rumbling . . . and the high-pitched screech."

"I'm not sure what you mean." Jordy looked away from Lisa, towards the unoccupied space behind her. "But I'm sure it's nothing to worry about."

Jordy patted Ben on the arm and headed towards the stairs to the fly bridge.

Ben leaned in towards Lisa. "He's lying, I reckon. He looked flustered, stressed out. Someone fucked up, and it was probably him."

4.

THEY DINED ON a liquid lunch, Ben, Lisa, Callum, and Cecilia, in the outdated and inelegant lounge. The two couples sat opposite each other at a table with cracked black vinyl bench seats and a stained and worn wooden tabletop. Outside the floor-to-ceiling windows, the sun beamed down on crystal water, but a strange formation of storm clouds rolled in from the south and threatened to bring back yesterday's gloom: a swirled mix of blackish purple, grey, and white—partially mixed paints on a sky-bound palette.

Sally, the third crew member, a young lady with long blonde hair pulled back in a tight ponytail, dismissively handed Ben his fourth beer over the bar. She excused herself, explaining that she would be back in a moment, before scampering comically fast across the room towards the stairs to the fly bridge. Ben took a sip from his bottle and returned to the group.

"Personally, I'm all for a few extra hours out here; it was insanely expensive for an overnight cruise," he said as he sat down.

"Worth it, in my opinion," said Callum. "No idea how they got the timing wrong, though. Someone's head is going to roll, surely."

Lisa listened to this and balked internally at the casualness of it all. She felt the anxiety throughout her body, and she could feel a thick air emanating from the others, too, but they seemed determined to brush it off. She stood and walked to the windows to get a better look at the impending cloud cover, which looked so unnatural, so hostile. It filled her with a strange dread, a paranoia brewing in her stomach and extremities, tingling, threatening to spread to her throat and heart.

"Those clouds look so strange . . . I'm worried about this storm," she said without turning around. No one replied, and the group went silent.

On the far side of the lounge, Aviators Guy and his wife sat on a small two-seater couch. He sipped scotch and she sipped white wine. They both looked out the windows silently and sullenly. Ben gestured towards them with his head. "They are a bit weird, yeah? Angry looking, not having a good time at all."

"They are fine, Ben," Lisa said as she sat back down. "Don't worry about what they are doing."

"I'm not worrying, just saying . . . a bit fucking weird, it's—"

"That's Stirling Falls," Callum interrupted, as he abruptly stood and walked to the window.

"That can't be right." Cecilia furrowed her brow.

"I'm sure of it," Callum countered. "Look at the way it splits off on the big rock in the middle."

"There are plenty of waterfalls along here," Ben pointed out.

"Not like that, there isn't," Callum said. "Look, I took photos in the evening when we anchored."

He pulled out his phone, unlocked it, and started scrolling.

"Here, look . . . it was getting dark when I took this, but you can see it's the same." He handed his phone to Ben, who placed it on the table. Lisa leaned over to look. Cecilia didn't seem to need convincing.

"I don't know," Ben said. "Sure, it's similar, but they all look the same."

"Wait," Lisa began, "look at the dip in the cliff at the top, and the way it slopes up on the left. He's right, it's Stirling Falls. But everything else looks different; the trees, the growth . . . it's all there but it's not quite the same, right? It looks even wilder and denser now."

"What does that mean if it is Stirling Falls out there? Are we going the wrong way? Back out to sea?" Ben asked.

"No, the falls are on the same side of the boat again as they were last night," Callum answered. "I remember we were heading out, and we turned as we slowed down, then we anchored with them on that side of the boat. We're heading towards the dock."

"That's impossible, right?" Ben asked.

Lisa pulled out her phone and swiped and typed increasingly aggressively until she gave up and dropped it on the table. "Anyone else got a signal?"

"No," said Callum, who still had his phone out.

"That's normal out here," Cecilia added. "I haven't had a signal most of the trip."

Ben kept looking between the falls and the couple in the corner who were watching the group with interest.

"Ben?" Lisa asked as she prodded him on the arm. But he ignored her, now fixated on the others.

Ben yelled across the room, "You guys need something?"

Aviators Guy smiled with contempt and Ben's body tensed at the sight. They held their gaze for a moment before Aviators Guy dropped the smile and spoke in a deep voice that travelled the length of the room with ease, "I told you before, we're lost. We are not in the right place."

"We're not lost, mate. You can't get lost on the fiord," Ben insisted.

"When did we last see another boat?" Lisa asked the group. "Yesterday, we saw them everywhere—other cruises, the big ones, and a few smaller boats too. I haven't seen a single boat this morning."

"Shit . . . me neither," said Ben."

"She's right," Aviators Guy agreed. "And you know why we haven't seen any other boats? Because . . . we are fucking . . . lost."

"What's your name, mate?" Ben asked.

"Richard, and my wife's name is Sarah."

"Alright, Richard, what do you know about this place? About Milford Sound?"

Richard didn't reply, just shifted in his seat, straightened his back, and looked Ben up and down.

"Not much obviously," Ben said. "Well, I'll tell you what I know. I know it's a fiord, and I know that it goes straight up and down and is surrounded by cliffs, so you can't get lost."

"Well then, genius, tell me why we have been going exactly nowhere. Tell me why there are no other boats . . . And what is that noise? You think this is all normal?" Richard countered.

"I don't know, you fucking twat," Ben replied with venom, and Richard rose to this, springing up from his seat and standing tall with an air of violence about him. He stood over six feet, taller than Ben and although both men were slim, Richard had a look of wiry strength about him, with big hands and pronounced shoulders. Ben flinched internally but gave away nothing on the outside; he was grateful for the distance between them.

"Jesus, Ben, take it easy," Lisa said, pulling him away and back to the table.

Richard sat back down without dropping his gaze, still wide-eyed and maniacal.

The boat slowed to a gentle pace and the groan of the engines further softened until they were barely moving at all. The black clouds from the south had swarmed the boat with alarming speed and it had become dark in the lounge. A banging sound rang out overhead, and then the *clank* of boots on metal as Sally jogged down the stairs from the fly bridge and entered the lounge. The group looked at her in anticipation, and she flinched when she noticed all eyes upon her. The boat stopped.

"What's going on?" Richard asked as she walked past him. Sally stopped, then turned and backed up a little so she could see the whole room. She glanced between the groups and swallowed.

"Well?" Richard prodded.

"I don't know," Sally said. "I wish I could give you an update, but I can't, and I'm sorry. We'll start moving again shortly, and I'm sure we will have everyone back at the dock in good time."

A pattering of heavy raindrops hit the boat. Then the clouds opened, and a downpour pelted the vessel as the winds kicked up and the windows became a grey blur. Everyone moved to the glass, lined up silently, staring into the murk.

5.

WHEN THEY PASSED Stirling Falls for the third time that day, Ben considered jumping into the water and swimming to shore. He shared this with Lisa, who reminded him that he would almost certainly drown.

Each pass of the falls had been preceded by what was collectively, and simply, referred to as *The Sound.* The repeated exposure seemed to sensitise them as it increasingly got into their blood and bones and played havoc with their nerves. They each felt dissociated and disorientated after. Callum likened it to emerging from a recreational dose of nitrous oxide. Ben still compared it to waking from a heavy, dream-filled sleep. The world around them appeared to be impacted too. The sky was closing in on them and the waters became increasingly black and volatile, surging and pulsing.

As the boat sat idle with dwindling fuel in the grey dusk, Ben and Lisa skulked in their room, attempting to stave off the anxiety with the remainder of a bottle of rum. They'd slipped off from the group when things had gotten increasingly tense; Lisa corralling her husband before he and Richard could come to blows.

Ben and Lisa passed the bottle between them and sipped and contemplated the lack of options that didn't involve traversing the frigid waters hiding deceptively deadly currents.

Ben took a generous swig of the bottle and exhaled noisily, as the wet *thud* of something hitting the water sounded out from somewhere outside.

"What was that?" he asked.

"I don't know," Lisa replied.

Ben stood sharply and exited the room. Lisa followed. They turned right and ran down the short hallway past several cabins before going up the carpeted staircase to the second floor. At the top, they immediately heard animated but unintelligible voices, and they joined the others who had already gathered on the front deck.

A single masthead bulb cast harsh white light across the bow, as a silhouette out in the water faded into the dark.

"Look, it's a small boat," Lisa said. "Looks like an emergency vessel.

The rumble of an outboard motor was loud in the otherwise quiet night. Ben and Lisa pushed closer to the crowd as the captain explained that his two crew members, Jordy and Sally, would take the life raft to the underwater observatory—the only point where a boat could dock along the sound.

"They will wait it out until someone comes to the observatory in the morning," he explained. "It's all we can do; everything on the boat is dead, nothing works."

"So now what, we just wait?" Richard asked, this time with his glasses holding back his thinning black hair, revealing beady, discontented eyes.

"We wait for help," the captain confirmed.

"Help? When they find someone . . . if they find someone, what exactly are they going to tell them? That we have been heading up the same goddamn stretch of water and going exactly nowhere?"

"They will say—" The captain stopped. Sagging, heavy eyelids, and hard lines suggested a man fading. He didn't finish his sentence.

"What makes you think they will get anywhere in that thing anyway?" Aviators Guy asked.

The captain didn't reply.

Richard continued. "There are two rafts, right?"

"Yes."

Richard nodded with pursed lips as he silently turned and left.

6.

NO ONE KNEW what time the storm hit that night, but Ben suggested to Lisa that it had only been dark a few hours. It had been raining on and off for a while, and at times very heavy. The word "storm" had been thrown around, but as the wind came in almost as violent as the immediate thunder, and as the gale converged and scudded cloud and rain between the mountains, and as the boat dipped, jumped, and danced, the true meaning of the word *storm* became apparent.

Ben vomited a stomach full of liquor into the small toilet off their room. He spat the last of his deposit, wiped his mouth, and flushed. It was a weak flush, and he wondered if the water tanks were running low. He left his mess, crawled into bed, and formed a drunken recovery position. Lisa slid under the sheets and mimicked him in a mirror image. She reached out and took his clammy hand. His eyes were wide and haunted.

"I can't stop thinking about it," he said.

"About what?"

"The accident on the way in, when we hit the bird. I keep replaying it in my head—the sound of the car hitting it, the noise it made, the screech . . . did it even make a sound like that? Am I making it up?"

"Ben, it didn't make a sound. You're imagining it."

"I thought so, but I can hear it. And I can hear its bones crunching in my head, over and over like it's in the room with us."

"There was nothing you could do. You know that, right? If you had swerved, you would have killed us," Lisa said, unsure whether she was lying just to comfort her husband.

"I was speeding, going way too fast," Ben admitted. "What if someone saw us? They are protected, yeah? What if someone saw me kicking it down the bank into the water?"

"No one saw us, Ben. And come on, we have much bigger problems to worry about now."

"It's burnt into my brain." Ben rolled onto his back and stared at the ceiling. "Tomorrow morning, if we are still fucking lost or whatever we are, the second the weather clears up, I'm jumping the rails and swimming to shore. I can't spend another day on this boat."

Lisa stroked his hand. Lightning flashed and lit the room, showing pale grim expressions. The couple gradually fell into troubled sleep.

Ben dreamed of having his arms snapped in three places. He was sitting on the back bench of the *Milford Guardian*, submerged in white frothy seawater that filled the boat's deck up to his waist and was swarming with various fish and aquatic life. The sun beamed down. The long, spindly, almost rat-like tail of an eagle ray whipped and breached and sprayed his face. The water ran into his mouth, and it was impossibly salty, drying out his lips and mouth instantly. He retched, and then he looked to the sky and watched the glorious blue above as it was torn apart from behind, revealing the darkest black he had ever seen. Shrouds of cerulean fell slowly to the earth like giant felled kites from miles above. Then the pain came. It started first in his elbows as they were hyperextended quickly and violently by an unseen force, and as he tried to resist, his forearms simultaneously snapped backwards, exposing jagged bone shards that tore through the muscle, fat, and skin. His elbows exploded dark red blood onto the bench and into the water around him, sending the frothy ocean runoff into a bubbling frenzy, like instant boiling. He felt something brush his legs. The two-metre shortfin mako shark that shared the tight waters with him latched onto his shin with serrated and triangular teeth, then he woke.

It was dark in the cabin. Lisa lay next to him, whimpering as if in a torturous nightmare of her own. Ben sat up and sweat ran down his nose. He ran his right hand along his left arm, which for some reason ached intensely, perhaps psychosomatically—everything was intact. As his breathing slowed, he became more aware of the noises around him, the water against the boat, and a scratching sound outside the door. He exhaled heavily and held his breath for a moment to listen.

Scraaaaape.

Scraaaaape.

The sound of something sharp digging into wood. And then tapping, a faint rapping like someone gently knocking on a door down the hall with the end of something sharp and narrow. He listened intently, trying to distinguish between the normal groans and creaks of a boat at night and the abnormal sounds in the hallway outside. Something else started up farther down the hall, like heavy breathing, an emphysema-like rattle of gravel and whistle. Inhale, exhale. Inhale, exhale. It got quieter as Ben thought he heard footsteps move up the stairs towards the lounge.

"Lisa," he half whispered as he tried to jostle her awake. "Lisa."

She cried out in her sleep but didn't stir. She continued to breathe heavily. Ben pulled the sheets back and noticed how sweat-drenched everything had become. He jumped out of bed and walked to the door. He put his ear to it but heard nothing. He opened it slowly and carefully and poked just his head out. The hallway was dark, but a row of tiny LED lights in the ceiling and the emergency *EXIT* sign at the far end gave just enough light for Ben to see that the hall was empty. He walked out into the space and just stood there listening. He heard nothing but the boat bobbing in the water. He looked at the stairs to the lounge and debated whether to investigate. After a few seconds of deliberation, he turned to go back inside the cabin and pushed the door open gently. A clanking sound rang out from upstairs, followed by a dull *thud*, right above his head. He stopped again. Another *thud*. He leaned into the cabin and pulled his black poncho from the hook on the door, then went back out to the hall. He pulled the rain gear on as he gently traversed the stairs in nothing but boxers and the hooded plastic cape.

He stopped at the top of the stairs and looked out into the open bar, which was dim but not totally dark thanks to more of the small ceiling-mounted LED lights. Traces of moonlight struggled to pierce the gloom outside the windows. Someone coughed nearby and Ben jumped. He jerked his head towards the sound and noticed a small bright orange light outside on the deck. He slowly walked across the lounge, eyes fixed on the glow, which darted up, held, then darted down again. Grey vapor plumed into the night and Ben recognised the silhouette of a man smoking.

The sliding door on the other side was slightly ajar just a crack; Ben put his hand in the gap and gently slid it open. This startled the man leaning on the deck railing and as he spun around, Ben realised it was the captain, holding a half-full bottle of vodka in his left hand and a cigarette in his right.

"Sorry, mate," Ben began, "didn't mean to startle you."

The captain didn't say anything, but he swayed and did a strange dip with his left leg.

"What are you doing out here?" Ben asked.

"Couldn't sleep," said the captain with a distinctive slur.

"Bad dream?"

"Nope, no dream . . . couldn't sleep. Can't dream if you can't sleep."

The captain pushed the bottle towards Ben, who took a heavy swig before handing it back. The captain did the same, then took an equally heavy drag on his cigarette.

"I don't even know your name," said Ben.

"It's Eugene, or Captain Sheridan, depending on your preference for formalities," he said, then placed the cigarette between his lips and extended his hand.

"Ben," he replied and shook.

Ben crossed his arms and pulled them in tight. His poncho flapped in the frigid breeze. A droning, humming sound was coming from somewhere lower in the boat and Ben stilled himself, tilted his head, and focused on it.

"What's that noise?" he asked, head still down.

"Discharge. The upstairs septic was full. It's emptying."

"Oh."

The captain took another heavy swig of vodka and passed the bottle to Ben, who did the same.

"I'm going to share something with you, Ben. I think I'm losing my mind."

"We all feel that way. What the fuck is going on?"

"No goddamn idea. I keep running us up the channel and we just keep ending up in the same place. Over and over. Like a loop."

"Could we go another way?"

"Another way? Like out to sea?"

"Sure, maybe follow the coast up north?"

"Not anymore we can't. Almost out of fuel."

Ben took another generous drink from the bottle and passed it back.

The gentle humming of the discharge gave way to a more invasive chugging sound.

"It's empty," said Captain Sheridan. "Excuse me, Ben, I'll see you in the morning."

He clumsily placed the bottle on the wooden railing, and it slid off into the depths.

"Ah, shit," said the captain. "Still plenty more in the bar. It's one thing we won't run out of—for a while anyway."

He took a final drag of his cigarette and flicked it into the water before walking off with his head in a cloud of smoke. He went around the side of the deck and into an open control box where he started tinkering.

Ben silently turned and left.

He crossed the lounge floor and started down the stairs, suddenly very aware that he was still half drunk. He staggered on the first couple of stairs and took hold of the handrail to steady himself. He descended with his eyes on his feet, stepped off the last stair with his left foot, and looked up. At the end of the hall, the silhouette of someone watching stopped him.

The dark and narrow hallway ran in a straight line, with several cabins off each side flanked by faded photos of local landmarks and birds obscured in the night. At the end, the emergency exit was wide open, and just outside it, the pale light of night barely revealed a heavily obscured, tall, and lithe figure that stood completely front on—just a still blackness. *A man*, Ben thought. But the low light and shadows played tricks, and he looked too tall and too hunched with a long neck and arms that floated out at strange angles from his body.

"Alright, mate?" Ben called out feebly. "You scared the shit out of me."

The man ignored him, and they faced off. Paralysed, Ben stood with one hand on the balustrade and his right foot awkwardly hanging off the bottom step. The shadowed man broke off and turned and as he did, his eyes seemed to reflect what little light there was before suddenly he was gone and the emergency exit swung closed on creaky hinges with a heavy *thud.*

Ben held his awkward position and struggled to steady his breathing. His heaving was loud in the quiet hall. His chest felt tight, like it was being compressed, and a ringing in his ears took over. The deep rumble started in his guts, then everything went black.

7.

THE PASSENGERS OF the *Milford Guardian* woke with the remnant of *The Sound* reverberating in their skulls—the scream of tinnitus as if a gunshot had gone off next to their heads—a violent alarm clock. Stomachs heaved and heads pounded.

Ben inhaled and gasped as he roused. It was morning. The dullest of daybreaks cut into the room via the gaps in the blinds. He reached across the bed and felt Lisa, who was still asleep. His breathing slowed, but the hot feeling of panic still coursed through his ribs and chest. He pulled the sheets off his side and slid out of bed. He shuffled to the window and lifted the corner of the blinds, bending and tilting his head to see outside. The dock wasn't there, only a dim, grey, and obscured morning that revealed little, but still quashed Ben's unfounded hope that somehow they might have magically returned to shore.

Images of the night before came in muddied waves: skies torn apart, noises in the hall, talking to the captain on the deck . . . struggling to separate dream from reality. *Captain Eugene Sheridan. I hadn't known his name before, so that part was real, it must be*, Ben thought. Then he remembered the watcher in the hall. He walked across the room and pulled the door open. Lisa stirred.

"What are you doing?" she asked.

"Nothing."

He stepped out into the hallway, but the dim passage was still. He heard a scattering of noises—low voices and thuds. Other passengers were stirring in their rooms and moving about upstairs. The emergency exit was closed. He walked back into his cabin.

Lisa was sitting on the edge of the bed. "I don't feel good," she said. "I had a terrible sleep. I think I might've had a fever—I had such strange dreams."

"Me too. I think," Ben said. "You look pale. You going to be alright?"

"Yeah, just give me a second."

"Okay . . . I think something is happening up there."

Upstairs, the morning had brought a thick fog that entirely shrouded the boat. Someone, presumably Captain Sheridan, had mustered a bowl of stale croissants and a pitcher of black coffee and placed both on a table in the lounge. A thick red extension cord ran from the back of a filter coffee machine and out the door to a generator.

Ben and Lisa each took a croissant and a paper cup of coffee—it was hot and felt good against cold hands. As they walked out of the lounge onto the front deck, they marvelled at what was merely a suggestion of the flanking mountains peeking through. They noted that the passengers slowly gathering on the deck were crystal clear in the drab and blanketed morning light—that somehow, the fog stopped cleanly at the edges of the boat.

Ben leaned his tired body against the rail. He extended his right arm into the gloom, and it disappeared entirely, like dipping into thick grey paint. He jerked it back as if something might take him.

Callum and Cecilia walked over from the other side of the deck and joined them.

"It's so thick I can't even tell where we are," Callum said.

"You think we moved overnight?" Ben asked.

"I don't think so," Callum answered.

The captain, haggard and sagging, took the centre of the deck.

"Morning, all," he said as he scanned the group. "Who's missing?"

"The girls aren't here." Ben continued. "And the other two, the couple, Richard and Sarah."

"Alright. Ben, would you mind going down and getting them? Hopefully Sally and Jordy have found help by now, but we need to start preparing for otherwise . . . as a group."

"Aye aye, Captain," Ben said, then turned and left.

"I'll come." Lisa volunteered and followed behind.

They dragged themselves back down the stairs to the hall with shuffling steps and stopped at the bottom. The emergency exit door swung gently on its hinges, open again at the end of the hallway but unobscured this time in the grey morning. There was no one there, but something about it triggered a sliding in Ben's guts nonetheless.

"What is it?" Lisa asked.

"Déjà vu. I came out here last night . . . but it's nothing. Come on," he said.

Ben stepped forward and the boat rocked. He braced himself against the walls of the narrow hallway. He walked towards the end, running his fingers under the faded framed pictures, calling out for the missing. Only distant seabirds called back. Lisa followed. A few feet out from the emergency exit, the wind slammed the door shut and Ben's already sliding guts crawled into his chest.

"Jesus," Lisa said, startled.

Ben struggled to open the exit door into the strong wind despite using his full body weight to push. He heaved and spilled out the door onto a small empty landing cloaked in the gunmetal fog. The occasional shape of a gull moved behind the mist, dipping and weaving and fighting the wind. Harsh cries were carried away as soon as they were formed. He let the wind pelt his face for a moment and then shut the door behind him.

"Nothing there," he said.

They turned and walked back along the hall, Lisa now in front. Two of the rooms had slightly open doors, just an inch or so, but no light showed through the cracks. They started there.

"What the hell is this?" Lisa asked, as she ran her right index finger down the door of the first cabin, feeling the deep ridges of a strange inscription in the wood, positioned just below her eye level, about six-by-six inches in size.

Ben pushed up against her, shoulder to shoulder, and examined the door.

"The scratching sound," he said.

"What scratching sound?" Lisa asked.

"Last night, I heard footsteps and a strange scratching sound. It must have been this; I heard this happening."

The inscription looked roughly like the shape of a classic keyhole, inverted, and with two horizontal lines through the middle and three dots in a vertical line on the right. The gouged flutes were crudely carved.

Ben knocked quietly and the door swung open a touch with a gentle *creak* of the hinges. There was no reply, so he held the handle to steady the door and knocked again, loudly this time. Nothing. He opened the door and felt around to his left for the switch. He flicked it on and in the gloomy orange light, he saw four bunk beds. Women's clothing lay strewn about on two of the beds and three suitcases were neatly lined up against the wall under the window. *The German girls*, he thought. The light dimmed and flickered, struggling for juice.

"They're not here," Ben said to Lisa, still standing in the hallway.

The wind had picked up and it whistled through the boat's gaps and openings, and the open cabin door creaked in syncopated symphony. They moved back up the hall towards the stairs and the other open door on the opposite side.

"Look," Lisa said.

The second door had the same indecipherable inscription carved into the wood. Ben didn't knock this time, just pushed the door open with his foot, as if to avoid handling something tainted. He stepped in, turned on the light, and found an empty room as expected. Two suitcases were lined up neatly against the wall. Ben picked one up, dropped it roughly on the bed, and started unzipping it.

"What are you doing?" Lisa asked.

Ben ignored her and flipped the top open, revealing neatly folded clothes and a plastic zip-up bathroom bag. He took it out and opened that too. He rifled around among hair gel and a toothbrush and toothpaste, then pulled out a small white plastic bottle and shook it, rattling the pills inside.

"They left everything," he said.

"Is this the right room?"

"I'm sure."

"They must be here somewhere."

"I don't think so."

They walked into the hall again.

"Hello!" Ben yelled out and banged on the wall next to him.

No one replied.

Back up on the top deck, Captain Sheridan was sitting slumped on the floor, leaning back against the window of the lounge. He was pale and sunken, and Ben remembered the half-empty vodka bottle from the night before. Callum and Cecilia were standing just back from the railing, staring into the dense mist.

"They're gone," Ben said to the group.

"What do you mean, 'gone'?" Captain Sheridan asked.

"I mean . . . they're gone, they're not there."

"Did you check everywhere?"

"They're not here."

"Did you have the right rooms?"

"Feel free to check yourself," Ben said.

With wide eyes, the captain stared past Ben and Lisa into the foggy void. His jaw tensed and released, tensed and released. He pushed himself off the floor and stood up stiffly. "Bastards," he half said, half spat as he started walking. "That guy, Richard, he asked about the other lifeboat yesterday. I should have seen this coming."

Captain Sheridan marched to the other side of the deck, passed Ben and Lisa, and went around the corner. He shook with a pent-up aggression, wound tight but jittery, as if expecting to find a particularly egregious transgression—something like his wife with another man. Ben and Lisa followed with Callum and Cecilia in tow. As they rounded the corner, Captain Sheridan stopped on a dime and the others bunched up behind him. The second lifeboat hung off the side of the *Milford Guardian* right where it should be; its bright orange frame as radiant as embers on the edge of the smoky fog.

"It's still here, so where did they go?" the captain asked.

"Did they swim?" Callum wondered aloud.

"No, they can't have," said Captain Sheridan."

"Why, though? Why sneak off in the night like that?" Lisa asked.

The captain turned and pushed past Ben and Lisa, then Callum and Cecilia. The group gathered again on the front deck. The temperature had dropped, and the hoods of jackets got pulled on.

Captain Sheridan went to say something but abruptly stopped, his eyes shifting back and forth.

An atonal sound started from somewhere, a rustling in the gloom, getting louder and closer.

"Is that rain? I think another storm is coming," Ben said.

Lisa looked to the sky. "It's birds," she replied.

A mass of birds began to circle overhead in dark clusters that came together, then broke and pierced the fog as they settled on the rails and roof of the *Guardian.* Hundreds, maybe thousands, of all sizes, colours, and species scattered about like sentinels, calmly observing the awestruck passengers. The stragglers circled overhead looking for space to land.

"What are they doing?" Ben asked, as the last of them bunched in tight among each other on the boat.

"They're watching us," said Lisa. "I don't like it."

Ben was poised to ridicule the notion that they were being watched until he saw the eyes flickering between the passengers with a noticeable flow—back and forth, like they were in sync.

Something thudded behind them, and they all turned. A large albatross had landed at the end of the bow. The huge white bird extended its wings in a span that far exceeded the height of anyone on the boat. Pinions with patches of ashy grey that turned to black on the tips. It brought those wings back in tight and stood tall, eying them all with olive-green eyes above a long, sharp, fleshy pink coloured beak. It settled its gaze on Ben. They all stood frozen and silent, transfixed by the great southern seabird as it held its pose.

The captain broke first, simply snapping off from the group and passing between Ben and Lisa with a slight brush of shoulders before continuing through the open sliding doors into the lounge. Ben turned to watch and winced when he was confronted by the flock as their pliable necks bent and twisted and flicked between the passengers under surveillance.

"I can't be here," said Cecilia. Callum grunted in agreement, then they both moved towards the doors.

Ben and Lisa followed. Inside, they all dispersed throughout the room. Lisa and Cecilia took seats at one of the tables. Ben and Callum kept going, past the girls' table to behind the bar, where they helped themselves to unmeasured glasses of whiskey. The captain looked briefly at this but said nothing.

When the great bird finally spread its wings and left the boat, all their chests loosened, although no one could articulate the feeling of dread that had accompanied the majestic creature whose presence would normally be a privilege.

No one spoke. The boat groaned. The cap of the whiskey bottle came off, clattered on the bar top, went back on, came off again. The sound of liquid pouring into glass tumblers was frequent. The smaller birds remained on the rails, visible through the window and audible via the scraping on the roof and the fluttering of wings. But they did not vocalise, as if they had said all they needed to say.

"I think we should take the lifeboat and get out of here," Ben said to the room.

"Where, though?" Lisa asked. "Do we even know which way to go? What if we go straight out to sea? Or into the rocks?"

"There must be compasses on board, something we can take. We just have to head southeast."

Captain Sheridan pressed his temples with his middle fingers. "They're fucked," he said, "all of them . . . We're fucked. Nothing works. We have to wait for the fog to clear, or we'll end up at the bottom of the sea."

The group went silent again and heads dropped. Lisa ran a hand through her hair and surveyed the space with an anxious energy. She looked at Ben from across the room, hoping for some sort of unspoken support for what she had to say, but he leaned on the bar top with an empty stare into the empty glass in front of him. She cleared her throat and spoke, "There were . . . uhh . . . marks on the doors downstairs."

All heads turned towards her.

"Marks on the doors?" Captain Sheridan echoed.

"Yes," Lisa said. "When we went to look for the others, we noticed that on both the doors of their rooms, someone had carved something in them, like a symbol."

The captain started to rise, pushing himself up against the wall he was leaning on. "What are you talking about?"

"Just on two doors, the two groups that are missing," Lisa answered.

"That is really fucking weird," said Callum.

"Why didn't you say something before?" asked the captain, staring first at Lisa, and then switching his accusatory gaze to Ben, who met his eyes briefly before looking away to his right.

Captain Sheridan marched a diagonal line from his spot by the wall to the staircase to the cabins. Callum joined close behind, followed by Lisa and Cecilia. Ben peeled his elbows off the bar and followed last.

Down in the hall, they clustered awkwardly in the tight space. The captain ran his fingers across one of the markings, then pushed past Callum and Cecilia and walked to the second door.

"What the fuck is this?" he asked the group.

"We don't know," said Ben. "It must have been done last night. I think I heard someone out here."

"Last night, like when you were walking about the boat in the dark?" Captain Sheridan asked.

"I was walking about the boat because I heard a noise. In fact, I heard someone scratching about down here and then head up the stairs, and that's where I found you," Ben explained.

"I never came down here. My sleeping quarters are upstairs," said the captain.

"Someone was walking about down here," Ben insisted.

"It was probably the ones who left in the night," said Callum. "Obviously they had to walk around to leave."

"Maybe this is some sort of code," Cecilia suggested. "Like they had a plan to escape, and they were communicating."

"Communicating? Why the fuck would you need to carve the door to communicate?" Ben asked.

"Hey, you watch your mouth, kid," warned Callum, his finger pointed right at Ben's face.

Ben stared back at him, the considerably larger man. "Where's your knife, Callum?"

"What?"

"The other morning, you pulled a knife out of your pocket, for cutting fruit or whatever. Where is it? Did you use it to carve these?"

"You brought a knife on the boat?" asked the captain.

"Relax, I forgot it was in my jacket. It's tiny."

"Show us," said Ben.

Callum reached into his jeans pocket, his eyes never leaving Ben, and pulled out the knife.

"Why do you have it on you now?" Captain Sheridan asked, but Callum did not reply.

"Can I see it?" Ben held out his open hand.

"Go right ahead," Callum said, then passed him the sheathed blade.

Ben opened it and inspected the blade, turning it over in his hands and looking for traces of wood dust and splinters. It was clean. He held the knife up to the door and ran it down the wood next to the inscription, leaving the tiniest of lines. He applied more pressure and moved the knife back and forth, digging with the tip of the blade. He worked on it for a while, five seconds at least. He made only a shallow and messy groove that looked nothing like the deep lines of the inscription.

"Satisfied?" asked Callum.

Ben ignored him. He pulled the blade away and examined the door. He moved the knife handle around in his hand and settled on a reverse grip with the blade edge on the inside. He twisted his fist, placed the point of the blade on the door, and hammered on the back of the handle with his other fist like a chisel. Tiny splinters flew off, but it still didn't match the form of the inscription, and the door moved and banged violently with each hit, a noise that would surely have woken all. He pulled the knife away again and looked around at everyone but couldn't read their tired expressions, other than Callum's obvious look of discontent. He folded the blade back in and handed the knife back. "I'm sorry. I had to be sure."

"Pull your head in, now's not the time to lose it," said Callum.

8.

THEY SAW THE day out back up in the lounge, alternating between solemn silence, useless theorising, and mindless chatter to keep their sanity from slipping entirely. And the drinking continued.

In what everyone guessed was late afternoon, a flash of lightning lit up the boat and the clap of thunder followed almost instantly. The sharp light sprawled over the lounge floor via the large windows. Parts of the fog had dispersed, and a dark purple sky fought its way through the gloom.

The group walked out onto the deck. The birds had gone, thankfully, but the bird-less sky, where visible, had become unusual and disturbing. Just off the bow where the fog was still the thickest, lightning flashed repeatedly, arcing right in front of the boat and lighting up the sky, accompanied by uncomfortably loud thunder. A heavy rumble of rain that could be heard but not seen continued. To the presumed west, there were bigger gaps in the fog where the strikingly beautiful sky pierced through with unnaturally vibrant shades of purple. The tips of green-dipped cliff faces peeked through.

"What is this weather?" asked Ben, a distinctive slur forming from the liquor. "I take it this isn't normal?"

"This is pretty fucking far from normal," said Captain Sheridan.

"Where are we?" Lisa asked, but no one answered.

The light shifted again as the shades of purple seemed to oscillate, and the sky in between the fog tore itself apart, revealing only the darkest black. A chorus of gasps rang out, highlighted by Cecilia's scream. Flashbacks of fever dreams came to Ben, and his muscles shook and twitched. For a brief moment he thought he might piss himself. A seagull speared through the sky in front of them at high speed, and then just disappeared. Tiny traces of light fell from where it vanished, like embers falling from a burning log.

"Oh god . . . oh god . . ." Cecilia muttered over and over.

Lisa wrapped her arms around Ben and pushed her face into his chest. The black sky began to soften and merge with the surrounding blue, like liquids being blended and emulsified. Lightning and thunder carried on.

"Are we dead?" asked Cecilia, finally breaking the silence.

No one answered, but they all turned to look at her. She didn't react, only stared into the blue-black sky, shades of catatonia in her dark brown eyes, like someone struggling to understand a bad acid trip—tumbling into a state of psychosis.

Ben was struck with a feeling of instant contempt towards such a stupid question: *Are we dead? Come on.* But the anxiety-driven nausea in his stomach was at odds with the attempt at rationale in his brain and for a moment, just a moment, it made a lot of sense.

Callum finally put his hand on Cecilia's shoulder. "Honey, what are you talking about?"

"I feel like I'm dead," she said. "I'm not me anymore. I'm just a shell, something else. This isn't real, the world around us is all wrong."

"We're just lost," Callum said as he pulled her in and embraced her tight.

"Lost . . . everyone keeps saying we're lost . . . Lost where, goddamn it?"

Callum flinched as Cecila flipped from sobbing to near screaming. She muttered something about wanting to go home, then pulled away and retreated into the lounge. Callum followed and took her hand in his, and together they walked down the staircase towards the cabins. A moment later, an unintelligible scream rang out and a door slammed. No one on deck went to check it out.

They stood in a line: Ben, then Lisa, and the captain to the left, and they watched the sky eat itself.

"I think there is someone else on the boat," Ben said, still looking up.

Lisa turned her head to look at him. "What does that mean?"

"I mean it literally . . . I think that there is someone, other than the original passengers and crew, on this boat. I think I saw them . . . last night."

"Why are you just saying this now?" asked Lisa.

"Because I wasn't sure. When I came back to bed last night, there was someone standing at the emergency exit in the hall. But then *The Sound*, that fucking sound, rang out and I woke up in bed. I thought maybe I dreamed it. But seeing the sky right now, I actually did dream that, and now it's coming back to me and it feels different, but the thing in the hallway . . . I think it was real."

"Thing?" Captain Sheridan asked.

Ben paused at this, trying to construct something that resembled the obscure figure without sounding like a nut job.

"Like a person, alright. They looked like a person, but a tall and messed-up one. But I didn't get a good look."

"You been drinking hard?" said Captain Sheridan, somewhere between asking and telling.

"Yes, I have been drinking hard," Ben snapped. What have you been doing the whole time? Sipping on water?"

The captain ignored him and turned back to the sky. "It's getting dark," he said. "If there is someone on this boat, we'll find them now; there is nowhere to hide from me on my vessel."

9.

AT NIGHT THEY negotiated a watch, and the captain dutifully took the first shift. He stationed himself on the fly bridge and watched for signs of light in the murk, listening for boats or helicopters or anything that might mean salvation. He watched the defective instruments and prayed that whatever condition had rendered them dead would miraculously lift and revitalise the needles and readings, allowing him to establish a position and to call for help.

They had searched the boat thoroughly and found nothing. Ben had taken it hard and hit the bottle equally hard. Callum and Cecilia hadn't emerged from their room, and despite talking about it many times, neither Ben, Lisa, nor Captain Sheridan had checked on them. The newly-weds chose to stay the night in the lounge, shunning the claustrophobia of their cabin and the proximity to Cecilia's outbursts.

The fog had closed its gaps, and the lightning and thunder had subsided. Only a heavy rain persisted, hammering down on the boat and lulling Ben and Lisa into a drunken and disturbed sleep in their chosen corner. In the depths of early morning, Ben thought he heard the sliding door open as he tossed and turned in a feverish half-sleep. He lifted a dizzy head and saw nothing through fuzzy eyes, then drifted back to his semi-comatose state. Neither Ben nor Lisa woke to the heavy footsteps by their heads.

"Ben, wake up," Lisa said as she jostled his shoulder.

"What, what is it?"

"It's morning."

The air in the lounge was crisp, and their breath plumed in front of their faces. Ben sat up against the wall and pulled the blanket over him. The boat rocked gently, and a hint of a purple sunrise emerged through the fog.

"The fog is lighter," he said, looking out the windows. "Have you seen anyone else yet?"

"No. It's been quiet. I've done something to my neck from sleeping on the floor. It's bad—can you get the painkillers from the room?"

"Yeah, of course."

Ben felt the hangover kick in when he stood, but it didn't bother him as much as usual. It almost felt normal, expected. He found himself thinking about the first drink of the day as he shuffled across the lounge towards the stairs.

His chest tightened as he started descending; the cabins had become his least favourite part of the boat—heavily associated with nightmares, noises, figures in the night, and a loosening grip on reality. It was dim, always dim down there, especially since the main boat lights had gone out. But it was oddly light this morning. As he reached the bottom and looked down the hall, he realised the extra light was coming from the rooms. Every single cabin door was wide open, and the drab morning sun cut through from the rooms and painted crooked shadows across the hallway floor.

His heart lurched. It looked wrong. He walked past the first door on the left and glanced into emptiness. The blinds had been pulled and the fog appeared to be shifting outside, slithering like something alive. He stopped at the next door on the right; Callum and Cecila's door was wide open like the rest, pushed back against the interior wall, revealing an empty room. Ben leaned in and found the same strange keyhole inscription carved into the front of the door. He backed out into the hall.

"Callum," Ben called out. "You down here, bud?"

Only the boat called back with its usual creaks and groans.

"Fuck," he muttered out loud, and stepped cautiously along, listening for signs of life.

He made a little grunt as he realised their door had been marked too. He stopped and examined it. There were two symbols. One just like all the others, and a different one next to it: a rough circle with two crooked lines through the middle of it. He burst into the room, breathing hard. He swiped Lisa's purse off the bed and picked up the duffel bag, which contained clothes and sundry items belonging to both, then exited.

He yelled, "Hello!" to the empty hall, and when no one replied, he turned and marched back up the stairs. "They are gone!" he yelled from the landing.

Lisa, who was lying down again, abruptly sat up. "Callum and Cecilia?"

"Yup. And there are more of those symbols carved into the doors . . . on our door too. But ours was different."

"What do you mean 'different'?"

"It was a different shape. I don't know what that means, though."

"Maybe it's a good thing?"

"A good thing?" Ben mimicked her.

"We're still here, right?"

"What if being here is a bad thing?" Ben asked.

"Captain Sheridan . . . we need to find him."

"I don't even know where the crew sleeps on this boat."

"He might be up top still."

Ben pulled open the sliding door and the gust of air that confronted them was salty, metallic, and heavy.

Lisa stood in the middle of the deck and surveyed the surroundings, embracing herself with arms crossed and shoulders hunched. Ben whipped away and around the corner briefly, emerging again a second later.

"I think we should take the lifeboat . . . now. It's still there," he said.

"I'm not going on the fucking lifeboat."

"We agreed—"

"We didn't agree on anything. You suggested it and I said nothing, because it's a stupid idea."

"We can't stay here," Ben insisted.

"It's bad enough here. No way I want to be stranded, sitting out in the open on some tiny raft. The water is rough, and it will be much, much worse in that tiny deathtrap. If we tip over, we will drown."

"We won't drown."

"We might."

"What will happen to us if we stay here? Where are they all? Every single one of them has disappeared in the night. Not a trace, not a goddamn trace, just . . . gone. It's just us left. Whatever is happening, we're next."

"Let's find Captain Sheridan before we make any decisions," Lisa suggested.

"Fine."

Access to the fly bridge was via a tight winding staircase that started on the front deck, just off the side. They rounded the corner and stopped at the small opening. There was no door attached, and they paused at the foot of the stairs.

"I think I can hear him," Ben said.

They both heard heavy footsteps, followed by the sound of something being dragged across the floor.

"What is he doing up there?" Lisa asked.

"I don't know."

"Should we go up?"

Ben put his left foot on the first step but hesitated. "Eugene . . . you up there?"

There was no reply, but they heard a faint scratching sound, and the similarity to what Ben had heard outside their room two nights before chilled his blood. He grabbed Lisa's hand and backed away from the door.

"What's going on?" she asked as they rounded back onto the front deck.

Ben let go of her hand and backpedalled while looking up at the fly bridge window.

Lisa followed. "You see anything?"

She watched Ben's face as he ignored her, and just when she was about to repeat herself, his eyes widened and his chest visibly sucked inwards as his mouth gaped.

"Who the fuck is that?" he asked.

Lisa spun around and looked up.

Above and behind the glass, a tall profile, far too tall to be Captain Sheridan, approached the fly bridge window and looked down on them as they stared upwards into the rain.

"Oh my god," Lisa began, "what's wrong with their neck? It's so long."

"Hey!" Ben shouted at the glass. "Who's there?"

The figure did not reply but took another step forward, revealing an impossibly tall and exaggerated ectomorph frame, gangly arms and long rubbery neck, and what looked like white and pale grey skin draped in some sort of elaborate coat that hung dramatically from its appendages.

Ben grabbed Lisa's hand. "There is something very wrong here. We have to go now."

They broke into a desperate but muted run towards the lifeboat with legs tensed to combat the surge of the vessel, trying not to slip on the wet boards. Ben put his arm around Lisa's shoulder, and they rounded the corner along the promenade. The lifeboat they sought looked beautiful and orange, but just beyond it, another figure stood waiting in a predatory pose. This one was constructed of dark greys and blacks, and without the streaky glass to mask its features, they saw clearly the most disgusting face staring back at them with seemingly hollow eye sockets harbouring contempt conveyed via the darkness in its orbital cavities. Lisa screamed like she had never screamed before, through ripping folds until the last projectiles of spit carried traces of blood.

The thing extended a bulbous head like a large and deformed human skull draped in rotted velvet, then it shrieked back at her from a small and sharp black beak protuberance that housed rows of saw-like teeth. As it did this, it raised long and leathery black arms draped in ancient ebony feathers with hints of reflective dark green.

When the shrieking stopped, they realised that they had just heard a milder version of something resembling *The Sound,* and as the ringing in their ears subsided and the brain-rattling confusion gave way to panic, the thing took a step towards them on powerful yet lissom legs.

They turned and ran, but on the other side of the deck, the second one—its paler counterpart—had reached the bottom of the fly bridge stairs, and it commanded so much space in front of them that they had nowhere left to go but back towards the narrowing bow. Ben grabbed Lisa's arm, pulled, and together they turned and jumped overboard, metres down into the dark frigid waters that instantly took their breath away.

"Stay close!" Ben yelled. "Swim!"

Their jeans got wet and heavy, and Lisa's sweatshirt stretched and sagged under the weight. Stroke after stroke, they made sad progress and prayed that they were heading towards shore and not the centre of the fiord where they would certainly drown. When a few minutes later Ben's hand brushed something sharp, he grunted in frightened disgust and then realised what it was.

"I felt a rock," he said. "Keep going!"

The fog thinned a touch and in the near distance, traces of green cut through. When they found land, joyless laughter that verged on maniacal rang out as they crawled onto a small and awkward shoreline rife with driftwood and debris, where the scrub grew to the water's edge and hunched over it like lapping animals.

"We made it . . . We were that close the whole time," Ben said through wheezing gasps.

They turned and looked behind—if something followed, they would see nothing until it was right upon them. In front, they faced a steep cliff covered in thick and difficult flora.

"We have to keep going," Lisa insisted.

"It's straight up."

"We have to follow the water as close as we can, on the lower parts."

They set off into thick growth with the cliff face to the left and the fog-draped water to the right.

"What the hell were those things, Ben?"

"Just keep moving."

"Am I going crazy? You saw what I saw, right?"

"Yes."

"How do you know this is the right way?" she asked.

"I don't."

Beneath the spreading shadow of the mountains and wearing clothes still as damp and heavy as their hearts, they walked through stabbing branches and over slippery and rotten undergrowth. Conversation was reduced to periodic whimpering. They didn't get far before the landscape shifted and the vegetation was replaced with rock that climbed violently straight up into the sky, as the brutal cliff pierced directly into the water.

"There's nowhere to walk. We're stuck," said Lisa.

"We have to swim . . . or wade if it's shallow enough, as close to the cliff as possible."

They stepped down into the water and their bones ached. Ben slipped and went under, revealing the water's depth, then scrambled back to the surface. Lisa sobbed and shivered as she, too, plunged fully into the water. They alternated between swimming and resting against the cliff face, bobbing like fleshy beached buoys.

"We're going to die out here," Lisa sobbed.

Ben said nothing.

The swimming became less and the resting on the rocks became more, while the cold became unbearable. When Ben felt like he could go no further, Lisa stopped and pointed at something.

"What's that?" she asked. "Ben, there is something out in the water."

He turned his head to look at the silhouette. "It's a boat. Jesus, it's a boat. Hey! Help!" he cried out while they swam towards it.

As they approached, they recognised the first lifeboat that had set off at what felt like an age ago now, empty, just bobbing in the current. Ben struggled to pull himself in and collapsed heavily on the floor before getting up and pulling Lisa in, who also flopped in a heap. They lay together for a moment and panted heavily.

"What happened to them? They didn't get far," Lisa said.

"Maybe they did, though . . . maybe we're close. The boat could have been pulled away from the dock by the current."

"There's a box." Lisa pulled herself up, crawled to the end of the small vessel, and flipped the catch on a black plastic trunk. "Thank god, there are emergency blankets in here."

They stripped off their wet clothes and hung them over the side of the raft, then they each wrapped themselves in two of the foil blankets and huddled together on the plastic bench.

"I feel warmer already," Lisa said.

Ben left her side. "I'll try the motor."

He struggled for what felt like forever to them both as he cursed and pleaded with no success.

"It's out of gas, or broken, or something. It's no use," Ben lamented.

"Are you sure you're doing it right?" Lisa asked.

"Yes, I'm sure," Ben said, his voice full of defensive snap. "It's not going to work. Maybe there are oars."

They scanned the boat for compartments that might hide oars but found nothing.

"We're stranded," Lisa said.

"We're safe for now. Someone will find us."

"We have no food or water, and this fog—"

"Just try to relax, someone will find us."

"Someone . . . no one has yet. And what if it's not help that finds us, what if—"

"I don't want to talk about those fucking *things*."

They huddled together and watched for signs of movement or light as they listened to distant waterfalls. Each time a bird sang they tensed, and their hearts dropped into their stomachs. As the day got darker, they slumped down onto the driest part of the boat's floor, lying awkwardly between the benches, and closed their eyes.

10.

THE GODS SHOOK out their coats and shredded the fabric of time with weathered talons. Shrieks rang out across the land and scrambled the neurons of man. Behind the great blue above lay the black. Behind the black, a knowing pair of eyes watched all and decided the time of the germs was up. One by one the rotten eggs would be culled; the exponential growth of the infestation would be halted. The captives were to be strung up. The water would claim itself back. If the rest of the world were to rot in putrefaction, then *The Sound* would stratify and revert to the old.

It was time.

11.

BEN WOKE TO the sound of more scratching, like something sharp along the boat's floor. His first sight when his eyes focused was Captain Sheridan's guts.

He was back on the top deck of the *Guardian*, face to face with the man who was gutted and hanging from the canopy, strung up with blue and white striped polypropylene rope wrapped around his neck and body. His dead eyes were open and dripping, battered, pecked, and chewed. The wound that travelled from his throat to his mangled penis had been jammed with rubbish and debris from the boat, food wrappers, and soft component plastic. Out of the wound stretched what looked to be his large intestine, pulled taut to Ben's right and pinned to the canopy's frame with a large, almost fossilised-looking claw. On the left, his crudely removed feet had been tied together with fishing line and hung from the top of the canopy like a pair of sneakers over power lines.

Ben's choking scream caught in his throat, but as the two figures approached from either side, it released in hyperventilating gasps.

The darker one stood to the right, its matted feathery coat and leathery limbs clearer now. The putrid, skin-shedding skull bobbed and peered at Ben. The other stood hunched on the left, a similarly monstrous figure, except white and grey with black accentuations, and eyes that were not sunken holes, but bulbous olive-green things that rolled in its head and looked right into Ben's essence. Ben went to run, but ropes and fishing line held him firmly to a metal chair, cutting into his naked body.

"Where is Lisa?" he screamed.

"Safe," said the pale one.

Its voice was just an unintelligible groan, saturated with a polytonal mixture of deep-throat gravel and high-pitched static that made Ben want to vomit. Yet somehow, he heard the words in his head, like they were being planted in there, whisper-like but crystal clear.

"Where?"

They ignored him.

"Where the fuck is she?"

The pale one answered as the other just stared with its ocular cavities above a gaping beak, "She has a job to do. You will be reunited shortly."

Ben's eyes returned to the gore in front of him. "What have you done to him?"

"Justice."

"What does that mean?"

The dark one extended its wings and hissed at Ben, causing him to recoil violently, the fishing line digging deeper into his skin.

"Please . . . let me go!" Ben blubbered, spittle flying from his mouth and running down his chin.

"It's too late, the trial has begun," said the pale one.

"Trial?" Ben repeated. "I don't understand."

"I think you do, you have dreamed of this, your actions haunt you. But remorse is not enough."

"Wait . . . wait." Ben squirmed in his ropes. "Is this about the bird I hit, the albatross?"

"The death of one of ours," it confirmed.

"I'm sorry. Please . . . it was an accident. What are you going to do to me?"

"That is the question: what will we do with you?" said the pale one.

"I'm sorry, just let me go. Please, I'll do whatever you want."

They said nothing, just breathed loud and sickly, whistling breaths.

Ben looked at the ground. The runoff from the captain's stumps was pooling around his own feet, and he further withered into a blubbering mess. "What did you do to hi—"

The pale one's voice rose in an anger that exaggerated the grit in its throat as it cut Ben off, "The man you call 'the captain' harboured criminals . . . foul people who mocked this place and our traditions. Over and over, they fed our kin with trash and spit and vomit. Their waste filled the waters, and the waters filled our bellies, and now the man has lost his. He entertained them, laughed with them, and took their money, with the audacity to do this aboard a vessel named the *Milford Guardian.* Now he is dead, and he guards nothing, and his marrow will nourish the water."

"Monsters" is all Ben managed weakly through hyperventilation.

"Monsters. So obtuse, so righteous. So removed. This is our world . . . *was* our world, until the germs showed up and we had to create the barriers to separate ourselves, retreating from our own homes while we watched you ruin everything. The toll . . . the toll on ours, yet you call us 'Monsters.' Carcass after carcass, you are death, you are destruction. No more. It is the accumulation of years of wretchedness that drives us. But . . . aren't you special . . . the one who triggered the revival, the final nail? You should feel privileged; few get to see behind the veil. The curtain is slowly being lifted, the old world will hide no longer, and you are one of the few lucky enough to come to our side, to see the arrival as it happens."

Thunder rumbled in the distance, and flashes of lightning cut through purple heavens where the blue sky above clashed and melted into an otherworldly canopy. A strong smell made Ben gag—salty ocean water mixed with the iron-infused stench of the disembowelled man, like a fishmonger and an abattoir in one.

He lowered his head and spoke into his chest, "I saw its eyes . . . when it looked at me. They were so different, knowing, like they were pleading to me. It was one of you, wasn't it?"

"We have been travelling between the layers for centuries. So it was no surprise that she was there. But on that morning, you struck one of us in your disgusting white petroleum vehicle. So young, so vulnerable . . . Mine." The pale one continued. "I saw you, and I saw a man who could have done something but instead dealt in broken cartilage and ripped remiges, and then in self-preservation and cruelty. You drowned my offspring in the river before I could do anything. So, I ripped the sky open just to keep you here, bring you through to our side to observe . . . assess. It's done now. No more talk."

"What are you going to do to me?" Ben whimpered.

"It's already done."

"You going to butcher me, too, huh?"

"Yes . . . but not yet. I want you to feel something first: the experience of being . . . discarded."

12.

AS THE HARSH sun beat down on Ben's burnt and blistering skin, he wondered what was going to kill him first: the dehydration or the multiple fractures in his arms that had them sitting crooked at his sides, like floppy flesh sticks that had been pounded and tenderised. He could only imagine the internal bleeding.

He sat hunched over in a small tin dinghy, barely large enough to hold him. All around spanned an endless and still ocean that belonged to him and him only. Birds circled above, squawking and crying out. *They are mocking me*, Ben thought. His stomach cramped again, pulsing and heaving. He had vomited and vomited until there was nothing left and continued to dry heave until only the bitterest of bile came up. He groaned weakly, a croaky moan from a dry and ravaged throat.

He could feel something on his head, the weight pressing down and making it dip. The rough edges pushed into him where his head had been forced inside the object. His vision was obscured and imposed on by the contours of the bone—the ancient moa skull from the giant and extinct flightless native bird that had been forced upon him as some sort of ceremonial and symbolic torture. Vomit clung to the underside of the beak and invaded his nostrils.

The thirst attacked him. Words bounced around his head like pinballs: The last conversation with Lisa, in the raft, what were his last ever words to his wife? Her last words to him? The gravelly grit of the voice of the creatures. Was that real? The delirium took over and unconsciousness threatened again. He pondered the thought that maybe he was just lost at sea, and the dehydration was making him hallucinate. *None of that actually happened? Maybe someone will find me?*

Then . . . clear and articulate, the words "Enough, it's time" came from somewhere behind him, and he knew it was very real.

13.

LISA SAT ON the deck of the bow and watched as they prepared the scene. The powerful limbs worked carefully, meticulous and refined and not what one would expect from those Lisa had essentially come to know as crude gods. Horrible and frightening, yes. Creators, no, but gods nonetheless—watchers, guardians, controllers of a realm, and now, architects of a future state. She processed this with what was left of her dwindling lucidity.

The darker one turned its head violently towards her as she sat and watched. *Where are its eyes?* she thought.

Lisa had been granted passage, left alive to speak, to represent. A chance to plead a case, just like she had always dreamed. She was giddy with excitement.

The thing turned its head back to its work and inserted a talon into the carcass. She couldn't tell whose at this point. A fly buzzed in front of her face. She swatted at it and marvelled at the size. The smell had attracted swarms of them. Lisa's nostrils burned with the intense malodour—

some of the meat had been butchered well in advance and started to turn.

The thing flicked some more discarded offal to its left with its feathered arm, and the gulls hammered down from the sky and took it.

14.

NO CRUISES HAD left the docks since the *Milford Guardian* went missing. Search and rescue boats had been plentiful, as had helicopters. The docks themselves, the visitor's terminal, and the facilities were not unoccupied, however, as the abundance of police, media, staff, and other bloated teams of officials went about their work with a baffling futility. The boat and its inhabitants had, as the headlines posited, vanished.

Lisa stood on the bow of the *Guardian* like a decrepit figurehead. Her red matted hair blew in all directions. Her sagging clothes drooped with the white weight of saltwater streaks and reeked of perspiration and piss. But the odour was masked by the metallic tang of the sculpture behind her.

Once more, the sky tore open, accompanied by *The Sound*, and this time the *Milford Guardian* finally returned home.

The view from the docks was limited by the curved line of the cliffs around three hundred metres offshore. The boat traversed the corner quickly, creating a panicked scene as people rushed from inside the terminal and the upstairs offices to watch the boat's approach.

The helicopter pilot above who'd been completing another routine flyover would've sworn the *Guardian* appeared from nowhere, and although he would not have been lying, he was wrong. It came from somewhere . . . from behind the veil.

As the vessel approached the docks, two uniformed constables prepared to board a small police motorboat and meet the *Guardian* in its approach. After one of the officers dropped his binoculars from his wide eyes and passed them to the other without a word, the decision was made to hold their position on the docks with weapons drawn.

The commotion drew all from inside the terminal, where employees, search and rescue teams, and friends and families had made base. As the boat approached, their disgust rang out in pulsing waves of dissonant screams and sobs.

The *Guardian* did not slow as it approached the wharf, and the gathering crowd began to back away as it was evident there was going to be a collision. It hit the wharf hard, the front of the boat bending back the metal railings before the vessel came to a grinding halt. Those gathered on the dock stumbled, at least those who hadn't already turned and fled or fallen to their knees in despair.

The missing had returned and been placed on display. In their death they had been ranked, and the torture had been in accordance. Callum, Cecilia, Sandy, Jordy, Richard, Sarah, and the three German girls had been rigged up like symbolically gored flags along the lounge windows in an alternating wreath—right way up, upside down, right way up—switching between strung around the ankles or around the throat. All had been slit at the stomach. Above, hanging from the smaller fly bridge windows, Captain Eugene and Ben had been elevated as the main focal point, in all their chewed eyes and slit belly glory. Ben still wore the skull of the moa. The guts ran down and joined the others' runoff, and a cocktail of bodily fluids pooled on the deck. Lisa stood in it, sloshed in it, still at the front of the bow.

She ignored the shouted instructions of the police and the weapons pointed in her direction. She smiled and addressed the crowd, "No, it's okay . . . it's okay. Everyone calm down. Calm . . . please. No need to be alarmed. My god, it is beautiful, so beautiful, so bright. You will see. I was saved so I could pass on their wonderful message. They don't have to hide anymore; the time of the veil is over. The curtain will be lifted, and the worlds will be together again. They are coming. They spared me with grace and with wisdom to pass on the message."

Lisa smiled with a knowing smugness. She observed her audience like a lawyer does a jury; she was well prepared and had them captivated. She brushed the sides of her jeans, flicked her hair, and then ran her fingers through it until it lay straight down over the sides of her face.

The crowd shifted nervously. In the near distance, the helicopter whirred as it closed in on the scene with urgency.

"Okay," Lisa said. She blew out a long breath like she was steadying herself under some sort of orgasmic pressure.

"I can hear them . . . they are speaking to me again. They say . . . everyone must leave. Leave now, or else . . . Oh, I see. Here it comes, leave now or drown."

As she said this, the water in the bay started receding violently. The *Milford Guardian* dipped heavily, and Lisa slipped and grabbed hold of the railing. She started laughing, almost uncontrollably.

"Oh fuck, tsunami!" someone in the crowd shouted, recognising the pattern of receding water.

Lisa abruptly stopped laughing and screamed, her bottom jaw protruding in a violent underbite with bloodied spittle, "Leave now or have your belly split like us before being fed to the water!"

Above, the sky darkened into shades of rich purple, as if being injected with dye—a wretched cosmic tapestry, the colours seeping through the fabric of the heavens.

Lisa stared catatonically as the crowd dispersed in a panic. The sounds of engines starting and cars accelerating aggressively dominated, followed by yelling, much yelling—fighting to get to safety. Lisa watched. Behind her, the badly broken-down bodies of her husband and the others dipped and weaved. She heard the voice of Ben in her mind. *You still want to move here?*

She let out a little laugh, just a two-syllable chuckle. *Ha ha.* She looked out at the water behind her, now swelling and coming in fast in the distance. Above her, seagulls swarmed and black clouds rolled in alongside the mountains. She heard what sounded like a distant, high-pitched *squeal* and smiled.

www.ingramcontent.com/pod-product-compliance
Lightning Source LLC
LaVergne TN
LVHW050938080826
845145LV00004B/1320

* 9 7 8 1 0 6 7 0 7 0 9 6 0 *